AF471621

VAMPYRE THEATRE

by

NANCY KILPATRICK

Baskerville Books

First Edition 2019

Cover Design: Istvan Kadar
Interior Design: Caro Soles

ISBN: 978-0-9813249-4-4

Acknowledgments

I am grateful to the people dear to me for friendships that endure, with all that that involves. Several people aided me in moving this book from manuscript to e-publication, including: David Dodd, Heidi Goode, Jason Graves, Rick Chiantaretto, Sam Reeves, and my editor Lloyd Penny. Special thanks to cover artist Istvan Kadar for his exemplary work. And to Baskerville Books, publishers of the print edition, for making that format possible.

And then there is you! Vampire fan...you're the Best!

Table of Contents

Praise for *Vampyre Theatre*

"I am always happy to encounter a Kilpatrick offering that I have not yet read. The characters are well steeped in theater history and the writing is seasoned with fitting lines from famous dramas...a quick read with sexy and interesting characters. I recommend *Vampyre Theatre* as an enjoyable, contemporary vampire tale. It is engaging and well written."

Elaine Pascale, Reviewer
Hellnotes

"All of them [characters] were gifted with fascinating personality aspects that absolutely hooked the reader. Excellent stuff."

Andy Boylan, film and book reviewer
taliesinttlg.blogspot.com

Vampyre Theatre

Act I

Passion Play

"I'm looking for a man."

Neanderthal eyebrows lifted. "You're in the right place, babe."

Sweat scent rode the cigarette smoke and Cheryl found herself sucking straw-sized breaths through her mouth. "His name's Nightshade."

The bartender paused a heartbeat before nodding to the furthest corner.

Green cone shades illuminated the felt on each of the dozen pool tables, islands of light amid the dense gloom.

As she walked towards the furthest table, Cheryl felt eyes like laser beams scan her body, stopping in places of preference: her thigh-high skirt, the bare-midriff red T-shirt. No one said a word; they didn't have to. She wasn't unfamiliar with macho environments, although she had never felt completely comfortable. She always felt alone.

A game was underway in the corner. While one man leaned over the table, another seven clung to the darkness near the wall. A stack of paper money balanced precariously on the edge of the wooden pool table.

The sandy-haired man was just about to make a shot when Cheryl's heels stopped clacking on the hardwood. He turned as if the silence was noise, said "Fuck!" angrily, dusted his cue tip with blue chalk, and then assumed a classic pool player's stance.

His cue pushed forward fast. It struck the black ball too hard at the wrong angle. The white spun crazily and then dropped into a pocket. He sent a murderous look in Cheryl's direction as he retreated to the wall.

She folded her arms across her chest, feeling both guilty and defensive.

Someone materialized out of the shadows. Tall. Lean. Long hair tied back, as black as the eight ball. His dark denim jeans and open black leather jacket fit his form like the skin on a snake. A cross earring glinted in one lobe. She saw white letters down the front of the midnight T-shirt:

+A–
+B–
+AB–
+O–
Universal Recipient

Drama, she thought, then modified her judgement: *melodrama.*

He stalked the table, circling it twice with sexual grace, eventually stopping at a corner so that he faced her directly. All eyes were on him. In fact, most of the room had paused to watch.

He lay the cue ball behind and to the right of the head spot, and then dusted his cue tip slowly, the motion sensuous. He leaned low across the felt, the leather of his jacket crackling softly in the now-quiet room. The cone light brought out a translucent quality of his flesh. Shadows highlighted cheekbones and a strong chin. *A handsome corpse*, she thought, and he flinched slightly as if she'd said that aloud.

He created a bridge with his right hand and laid the stick across it between his thumb and first finger. Cheryl noticed the cue's handle. Mother of pearl inlays glittered beneath the single bulb. From everything she knew about him, that was just his style.

The shot was a perfect set up. Cue ball. Eight ball. Cheryl's groin. He hunkered down behind the white, eyes close to the felt, and adjusted the bridge unnecessarily, going for drama again. She watched the cue ease back, the tip aim at the bottom of the white. The air cleared and the space between the two of them hollowed into a tunnel where time hovered.

Suddenly, his head shot up. Yellow eyes soldered into her green ones, his the color of flowering buffalobur, the nightshade family. He winked at her and at the same time his lips twisted cynically downward.

Mesmerized by his stare, she heard, more than saw, the cue slide as if in slow motion. The cue ball started forward fast, then abruptly stopped dead in its tracks. It shifted direction and spun under itself across the table. White barely tapped black. Black rolled willingly into the hungry mouth waiting to devour it.

Reality fractured as if one of the green glass shades had

crashed to the floor and shattered. Noise. Movement. Balls clinked, smoke clotted the air. He was already unscrewing his cue, returning the two halves to the case, pocketing the money. Walking past her.

"Nightshade!" she called sharply.

He stopped but did not turn.

She watched his broad shoulders tense as she said, "Aleron sent me."

Now he turned, an animal focusing on prey. A hungry animal. Ferocious. Before he could say or do anything, she said quickly, "My name is Cheryl. We need to talk. In private."

He handed over his case to the bartender in exchange for a key to a store room. He held the door open, and Cheryl entered first. She walked toward the antique pool table in the middle of the small room, surrounded by four walls of empty beer cases. He followed her inside, closed and locked the door.

"Turn on the light!" Cheryl said, feeling the threat of complete blackness.

As tense energy rushed toward her, she realized that coming here, onto his turf, was not such a good idea. She backed against the table, trying to avoid what she now realized was unavoidable, and braced for the inevitable.

His powerful vibration overwhelmed her. In the darkness, his lips brushed hers on their way to her throat. His incision was quick, precise, almost surgical. Painless. In no way dramatic. Obviously, he wasn't the type to waste time when he was hungry, even if he had plenty of time to waste.

Cheryl felt energy drawn from her veins, sucked up through her heart, down from her head. Cold silver light exploded on the inside of her eyelids, freezing her thoughts. Her limbs went glacial and numbed. She struggled to shove him away, but he was stronger, as she knew he would be. He could leave her near death. Vulnerable. Or worse. "Stop!" she pleaded, but the word was whispered, barely audible.

Finally, he did stop, not when she asked, when he was finished. As he moved away, she collapsed onto the pool table, the weakened rind of a fruit after the pulpy juice has been sucked out.

More light flooded her brain, a myriad of stabbing colors. At first she thought it was a hallucination from rapid blood depletion. But, the faint chatter, the clink of ceramic balls striking one another told her he'd opened the door; she was losing him. "Wait! Please," she gasped.

He closed the door. He didn't have to. She knew that. His energy was still impatient and as bright as hers had been before it faded and dimmed.

Cheryl propped herself up and looked in his direction. She could not see him, but knew he could now see her clearly in the dark. "I need help."

"Call a doctor."

"Aleron said I could trust you."

"Aleron lied."

"Before he died, he told me where to find you. He said to tell you he's calling in his chips. You owe him. Pay me."

He was on her before her pulse could move along the small amount of blood remaining in her body. She suspected if there had been any blood left worth taking, he would have yanked it from her veins and left her to the mercy of the mortals.

He grabbed the hair at the back of her head. His eyes glowed supernaturally, shooting yellow sparks at her in the darkness. His pale face flashed disbelief and pain, alternating with fury. She knew he and Aleron had been close, once, and suddenly understood why.

Whatever his face betrayed, his words belied those feelings. "Were you a masochist before you died, or did it come with the transformation?" He shoved her back against the table.

She heard a click. Instantly, white funnelled light from the shaded blub overhead rocked crazily around the room. Cheryl howled and covered her eyes against the solarlike glare.

"What did you expect?" he demanded. "I'd greet one of Aleron's castoffs with open arms? Welcome to my nightmare, sweet virgin of the dusk? I always wanted a child."

"Aleron said you can be cruel."

He laughed. The sound cut through her like a claw ripping its way down her backbone. "He should know." Teeth bared, he looked fierce. "He didn't teach you much about vampire etiquette before he bit it, did he? How unlike him not to foster independence. Maybe you should go nip Miss Manners."

He grabbed Cheryl and forced her to look at him. The

power he emanated was horrifying and beautiful at the same time.

"One, vampire baby: never, *ever* venture into the territory of another *nosferatu*. It's an act of aggression. What happens next is instinct. You just got a taste of mine as I got a taste of you. Got that?"

She nodded weakly.

"Two: we are a solitary species, in case Aleron didn't manage to convey that. If you should accidently wander into another's designated dining area, get the hell out as fast as you can. Am I making myself clear?"

She nodded again.

He looked at her with a combination of revulsion, pity and annoyance as he pushed her away from him. "How long?"

Cheryl braced herself upright against the table as her head swam.

"What?"

She felt his impatience like an assault. "What do you think I'm asking? How long have you been coming to pool halls?"

"I've been like this just over a week. Maybe ten days and nights."

"Damn!" He ran a hand through his hair. "Aleron was always a sucker, so to speak, for blondes. And brunettes. And redheads. So, why are you here?"

Cheryl crawled up onto the pool table so she could sit; she didn't have the strength to stand. She studied his vitality and wondered how he'd react if she asked him for a little blood, just to tide her over.

"Don't even think about it," he said.

"Am I so obvious, or can you read minds?" Her brain felt dried out, and the room was weaving worse than the light. She bent her head, trying to keep from passing out, and fell forward.

A hand like a wall stopped her body from plummeting and held her up. "I hope Aleron rots in hell!" she heard him say, accompanied by the muted sound of leather crackling.

The scent spread up her nostrils and down her throat. copper roses. She opened her eyes to see a river of rubies. He pulled her head to a slit he had cut into his chest, and her lips found the wound as easily as a nursing baby finds a nipple. She held his shoulders in a vice grip as she sucked.

Warmth flowed in, expanding out from her stomach and through her icy body, defrosting her. The metallic roses blossomed, and warm rain coated her flesh. Warm rain in moonlight and—

Suddenly, she was cut off. It was as though a silver knife had severed her into two sections, heart and head.

He shoved her away. "Greedy little leech. Don't expect to be invited back to any of my soirées."

She felt much better. Mind clear, body energized. She was still hungry. She watched him press two fingers to the wound near his heart. Within seconds, the bleeding ceased.

As he was slipping his T-shirt and jacket back on, she noticed defined muscles dancing beneath his skin. "Why did you help me?" she asked.

He turned away.

"I mean, you could have left me here to rot. Aleron said you might."

He turned and the look on his face was amusement. "Aleron said that, did he?" He threw back his head, opened his mouth, and roared with laughter. He looked like a wild, fanged animal, so self-satisfied that for once it let its guard down. His stained incisors glinted steel-strong, and were longer than Aleron's.

Cheryl's tongue felt in her own mouth: her eye teeth would grow. Aleron had assured her of that. In the meantime, she'd have to find another way to pierce skin, *if* she could bring herself to do it. All the blood she'd drunk had come from Aleron, and now Nightshade.

Again, his words said he was privy to her thoughts. "I suppose Aleron fed you with an eye dropper." His eyes turned serious and one side of his mouth pulled back in disapproval. "As of this moment, vampire baby, consider yourself weaned. Tomorrow night you hunt or starve."

The idea frightened her. She didn't know how to feed. Didn't know if she could even bring herself to do it. Drinking some blood from Aleron, and now Nightshade, was one thing, taking it from a breathing, pulsing mortal... Someone who was very much alive as she herself had been not so long ago...

He reached out and instinctively she ducked, but he only pulled the cord and shut the light. He crossed the room, opened the door and was gone.

Cheryl hesitated only seconds before jumping up to follow.

Nightshade had collected his case and was already starting down the steps to street level by the time she caught up. His hips held just the right amount of tension. His stride was long, his legs muscular and powerful in the tight black jeans, and she had trouble keeping pace. Aleron had assured her that her strength would increase over the years. What he didn't tell her, she had deduced: for a while—and she didn't know how long—she would be as fragile as eggshell, sensitive to impending daylight as an albino animal, volatile as a volcano in her needs. In fact, her hunger was outrageous by any standards she knew. She wanted food—no, *blood*—when she wanted it, and all other drives paled in the face of what she was quickly realizing was a compulsion. Not one she had any control over either.

Nightshade stopped beside a black Jaguar with tinted windows and unlocked the doors remotely. *This is probably where he seduces his victims*, she thought.

After they were both seated, he looked at her before starting the engine. "Better buckle up, darlin'. At least that's what I tell the warmblooded men and women who usually sit in that seat."

Suddenly, she was tired of being toyed with. "Look, if you can read my mind, just say so."

"Anybody can read your mind. Your heart's on your sleeve, and your thoughts, mundane though they be, are imbedded in your pretty little face like gossip in *Variety*."

Despite the insult, she felt a secret thrill that he'd called her pretty. She stifled that thought, though, in case he was aware of it. "Where are we going?"

"Nap time."

She was annoyed with him and stared straight ahead, not wanting to give him any satisfaction. Not wanting to give him anything. This old vampire/new vampire routine was growing stale. But, even as she thought that, she also felt surrounded by liquid exhaustion, a feeling much the same as when she used to dive into a pool and be engulfed by water. Pressed from all sides. Weightless. Alone.

When Cheryl opened her eyes, she was lying in darkness alone. She sat up and banged her skull against something solid. Above her head and on both sides she felt wood. She was in a wooden box. No, a coffin!

A panicked scream was just erupting from her gut when the ceiling raised and strong light poured in.

"Sleep well, my little seraphim?"

When she could tolerate the light enough to open her eyes, Nightshade's perfect features filled her range of vision.

"Let the hunt begin!" he said with a sonorous tone, walking away. Then, "Shake your booty, scream queen."

She sat up in what was a coffinlike box. It wasn't like any coffin she'd seen before, not that she'd seen many. Aleron hadn't slept in one, but he did require complete darkness. As did she. The rectangular box was big enough for two, and she was naked. "How did I get here?"

"You morphed into a bat and flew in your sleep." He stood, legs apart, hands on his slim hips, wearing a variation on yesterday's outfit, looking handsomely ferocious. "I carried you in from the car, how do you think?"

"You didn't sleep with me, did you?"

He raised an eyebrow, crossed his arms over his chest, and made a disgusted noise. "Aren't we being just a tad precious, princess of darkness, not to mention unnecessarily chaste? And ungrateful. I don't have a spare casket. I wasn't expecting company until the next millennium."

She hauled herself out of the box and onto a platform that took up most of the floor. Her clothes were next to the coffin. She felt his eyes licking her body and her nipples hardened as she dressed quickly, all the while looking around her.

The hardwood floor was a stage. A heavy scarlet curtain with tassels along the hem hung at the edge of the stage. Above, the high-domed ceiling was embellished with plaster flowers, leaves and classical figures. Blazing stage lights illuminated the entire area. Out in the darkness she saw rows of ornate velvet-covered seats. Other than that, the relatively small space was bare. "This is a theater!" she said astonished, slipping her skirt up over her hips, remembering that Aleron told her Nightshade had been an actor, and a good one, at least before he changed.

"No kidding. All the world's a stage, honey, and the play's the thing. I am the star of this farce." He crossed one arm over his midriff, extended the other above his head and bowed deeply. His body snapped upright. "And, you're the bit player."

"Why are you so hostile to me?" She turned on him, sick of his cynical jabs. Hunger was making her irritable.

He walked to stage right and flipped a switch. The platform with the coffin on it lowered into the floor; wooden floorboards raised to disguise the opening. Another switch clicked and stage-edge footlights caught her from below. She turned away and cringed to avoid the searing light.

"How did Aleron die?"

She'd been waiting for this question, but now that he'd asked, she didn't know where to begin. "It was out of the blue. Could you turn those lights off?"

"You mean it wasn't cancer? He didn't wither away? Fade to nothing from old age? How odd." Nightshade stalked her. She was intimidated by that same wave of power she'd felt the previous night. "Cut to the chase, honey. You might have all night, but I have plans to keep and miles to go before I sleep."

"There was a fire in the building during the day. The firemen came with their hoses, breaking down doors and windows and..."

He turned his back and walked away from her, his Doc Martens slamming the boards.

"He died instantly. I don't think he suffered."

He spun back. "*You* don't think he suffered? How the hell would you know, you fledgling twit?"

"Look, don't take it out on me. I didn't start the fire. I would have saved him if I could."

Before she could blink, his face was in hers. "How come you survived? Aleron had five centuries of experience under his belt. Seems suspicious to me."

"You don't think I did that to him? What possible motive could I have? He was my protector. He helped me adjust."

"He brought you over. Was it against your will, or did you grow up in the burbs loathing garlic and dying to sleep on dirt?" His face was cold, murderous. "How about revenge? You wouldn't be the first. Like I said, Aleron wore blinders."

"You hated him. Why do you care how he died?"

"I'm more interested in why you lived."

Cheryl was silent. She would never beat him in a word battle. Anything she said would be misinterpreted, twisted and used against her. Frustration mixed with vulnerability and she burst into tears. "I loved him! Maybe you can't remember love."

She sobbed into her palms, her body racked with the pain of loss. Cheryl had no idea she could feel so deeply about someone she'd known only a short while, but the bond was intense.

Through the agonized sounds that welled from her, she heard him say, "'Yes, I too can love.'"

She peeked through spread fingers. He was looking at her, but his eyes were really inward, remembering, she suspected, people from his long past. Maybe remembering Aleron. His face had contorted into an agony that made her sadness seem like a shallow emotion.

When he became aware of her close scrutiny, Nightshade's features altered like a shape shifter transmuting to a completely different form. "Bram Stoker's *Dracula*. The infamous count's rebuttal to the three vindictive bitches of the night who are struggling to justify their tryst with that cretin Jonathan Harker."

"Isn't anything important to you? Don't you take anything seriously?"

He came forward and then cupped her chin, looking earnestly into her eyes. "The wine of life, my dear, a pleasing script and a gorgeous cadaver."

She shoved his hand away. "I'm hungry."

"I'm sure you are. And you'll eat. Once you explain why you, too, were not barbecued."

She sighed and looked around the stage, wishing for a chair. She wasn't physically tired, more emotionally drained from this rollercoaster ride. There was no chair in sight. She considered perching on the edge of the stage, but the lights were hotter there and, too, she decided any weakness she showed would be used against her.

"Aleron made me sleep in a huge trunk at the foot of the bed. He slept under the bed. He said my skin was too raw for even electric light."

"And, why didn't the trunk incinerate?"

"It was cast iron on the outside, siliconed on the inside. Aleron said whenever he moved, he brought it with him. He said you gave it to him."

Emotion flickered in Nightshade's eyes and he turned away.

"Look," she said, "I know you and Aleron were close—"

"This isn't an airbnb. Get out and get it before it's contaminated."

He headed out the stage door into the alley. Cheryl followed, feeling nervous. This was a test, and she sensed it would not go well. Hunger swelled within her like a rush of sexual heat. She would not be able to resist, and yet she couldn't see how she'd be able to kill a human being.

She ran to keep abreast of him, asking, "Tell me about it. How do you do it?"

"Well, first you rent evening clothes—in your case a diaphanous gown—and a long cape. Next, you practise a hypnotic stare. Just be careful you don't accidently put yourself under. Then—"

"Come on! I'm scared. I've never done this before."

He stopped under a street light and looked down at her. Something about what she said, or her naiveté must have touched him. She wondered if he was reminded of his own beginnings.

Gently, he brushed a lock of stray hair back from her forehead. His fingertips lingered on her skin. His eyes softened. "It takes getting used to. You don't have to hit the jugular; any old vein will do. Just make sure you avoid severing an artery, or you'll have a corpse to dispose of. You don't have to kill them. If you go to the right places, most will give you some blood willingly."

"They will?" She could hardly believe it.

"My dear, 'The only way to get rid of a temptation is to yield to it.' Oscar Wilde. *The Picture of Dorian Gray.*"

"Look, I know you don't have to help me. I just want you to know how much I appreciate—"

He cut her off by walking away.

They reached a basement club, the battered, rusted sign outside identifying it as *Necropolis.* The dark interior was sparsely decorated, composed of huge amps blasting ear-shattering death rock, a machine clotting the air with fake fog, a near-blinding, disorienting, flashing strobe overhead. The space was packed with bodies, each looking like they'd just come off the set of a vampire movie.

Nightshade moved through the crowd easily—it seemed to part dramatically to let him pass—and stopped at the chainlink bar.

A redhead with one side of her head shaved, wearing electric purple lamé tights under a black leather mini skirt and iridescent Docs on her feet, threw her arms around Nightshade's neck. He grasped her hips and whispered something in her heavily-cuffed ear.

She gave Cheryl an up and down, leaned over and yelled, "Hiya, I'm Poppy."

Then, she turned back to Nightshade and nodded. He slipped an arm around her waist and led her out of the club. Cheryl followed like a faithful puppy.

Within two blocks they reached a rundown brownstone. The girl seemed drunk or high. She giggled all the way up the three flights of stairs, swinging her hips into Nightshade's and running a hand over his backside and between his legs. Inside the cramped apartment, she headed right for the cluttered bedroom, stripping the clothes from her body and kicking off her heavy boots as she went. Nightshade followed, but didn't undress.

Cheryl looked around. Cheap fabric covered the lamp next to the stained futon. A mishmash of items hung from the ceiling with no discernible theme: a mobile of hypodermic needles, a wind chime made of shotgun shell casings, three decapitated teddy bears hanging independently, an anatomically correct skeleton of a child—Cheryl hoped it was plastic. *This girl could have a disease,* she thought, scanning the filthy clothes and dirty dishes scattered around the room, not to mention the ferret skittering across the floor, wondering what, if anything, vampires are immune to.

When she turned her eyes to the bed, Nightshade's face was between Poppy's legs. The redhead writhed and squirmed and groaned as if she had lost her mind, yet managed to reach over and press a series of buttons on a music player. An old *Alien Sex Fiend* song screamed through the speakers, the loud, repetitive lyrics about being zombified.

Cheryl slapped her hands over her ears. This was unbearable! She didn't have to put up with this. If Nightshade wanted to screw some crackhead, that was his business, but Cheryl had better things to do. Once she got away from this insidious noise, she'd be able to think about what those things were. At least the music coated the acid jealousy searing her gut. Jealousy for who or what, she wasn't sure. She started toward the door.

An invisible beam galvanized her energy, forcing her

to turn back.

Poppy's hips rode the air, circling, pumping to the beat.

Nightshade turned his head and grinned. His eyes blazed magnetic sunlight. But, it was the crimson sunset smeared across his full lips and dripping down his long fangs that attracted her more.

Cheryl moved as if she were a hooked fish being reeled in. She crawled onto the bed. Poppy's nipples were hard pink nubs; Cheryl's mouth found one and pulled it up with her teeth. The girl groaned. Nightshade vacated his position, and Cheryl moved down Poppy's taut flesh, past her navel to the red forest.

His incision still flowed just above the clitoris, and Cheryl's lips sucked at the wound. Each mouthful of crimson fire plunged the girl into spasms of ecstasy. Cheryl drew fast and hard, feeling a flash fire spreading through her own genitals.

Suddenly, she was yanked backwards across the room.

"Bastard!" she shrieked. She tore at him, gouging his face, kicking, punching, tangling with him on the floor, spewing rage. *How dare he keep her from that fire!*

Nightshade was far stronger. He dragged her backwards out of the bedroom. Once they were beyond the prime scent zone, he pinned her arms behind her and pulled her hair until her head was back and her throat exposed. His hot wet lips pressed onto her skin, near a vein or artery, close to her ear. "Chill, baby, or I take it out of you."

The idea of the blood leaving her body sobered her fast. She panted and trembled, sweating uncontrollably. But finally, she calmed enough that he relaxed his hold, and then released her.

She gulped in air, trying to slow down and get a grip.

Through blurred vision she watched Nightshade walk into the bedroom. Her perception was off; she couldn't tell if he'd been gone a long time or a fraction of a second. When he came out she heard him say something like, "She'll be weak for a couple of days, but no major damage. Beginner's luck, but you need discipline, young one, even if you are teething. Learn to restrain yourself, or I'll restrain you, and if I do it, it won't be pretty."

On shaky legs she followed him onto the street. The night moved at triple speed, and then there were moments when time stopped. She watched an old man hovering in a doorway. He moved closer. Or did she move closer to him? His face lifted and his cheeks crinkled. She felt so linked with him. Soul connected. His eyes registered surprise. Pleasure. Fear. Suddenly, Nightshade was by her side, scowling, tugging her away.

His hand on her bare arm felt wonderful. She turned and looked up at his seductive face. When those gold fire eyes met hers, sparks flickered between her legs; she wanted him.

They were at the theater. On the stage. He raised the coffin and opened the lid. "Get in."

Panic seized her. "Why? It's early. I'm not tired. I'm still hungry, I—"

He stepped into the box and pulled her down with him and then closed the lid. She felt them descend. "It's too dark. I'm afraid!"

She heard a switch flicked. Subdued light filled the sides of his satinlined bed. His face, so near, so naturally necessary. Eyes like twin suns caught hers. "I'm hungry," she whispered again.

"I know," he said.

Lips grabbed onto lips. His hand slid under her skirt, up inside her. She felt liquid break over his fingers, and her body quivered as she moaned. She licked his chest and stomach and his hardening penis. He squirmed as her mouth controlled him. She tensed her lips and his flesh grew taut, straining.

He undressed, her T-shirt came up, her skirt was kicked down around her ankles. She crawled on top of him, letting herself slide onto him until he was deep inside her.

She propped herself up by her arms and arched her back as far as the confined space would permit. Her hips rode his. The folds inside her rippled and swelled with electrical tension. He pinched her nipple in much the same way she had nipped at Poppy's, and she moaned, astonished at the spiralling pleasure.

The orgasm exploded through her like a dynamite charge.

Shards of light sprayed past the edges of her skin, melding inner and outer realities. Her body went rigid before it went slack, and then she collapsed on top of him.

He was still firm inside her, his muscles tense, his eyes hungry for her. In one movement, he flipped her over so that he was on top, thrusting deep into her.

He bit into his wrist until the blood flowed, then moved the wound to her mouth. Her lips found the red river and drank. And then his teeth poised over her jugular.

Just before he pierced her flesh, he whispered, "That was only the first act, sweet vampire baby. Stay awake for the finale."

When she woke the next night, Cheryl found a sprig of flowering deadly nightshade in her hand. The coffin lid was open. Lighted votive candles in tall glasses lined the edge of the stage, casting a romantic *Phantom-of-the-Opera* glow over the shadowy space.

The theater was empty, she could sense that, or rather sense that Nightshade was not here. She was beginning to realize that the absence of living or undead defined what she experienced in the presence of both.

She felt incredible. Magnificent, really. Last night, when they made love, Nightshade had opened a new part of himself to her, as she had opened to him. He was vulnerable. Needy. He must have been alone for a very long time—Aleron said they hadn't been together for a century. As strong as her bond with Aleron had been, her connection with Nightshade felt more real. Sharing their bodies in so many intimate ways—sharing the blood—it was a union she had not dreamed possible.

Cheryl was startled by what she felt for him. The attachment ran deep and wide, as though they were soul mates, lost and wandering through time, who had found one another. And, she was acutely aware of one other thing: blood was no longer her only obsession. She wanted sex. With Nightshade. And she wanted a lot of it.

She dressed quickly and waited, but when he didn't turn up and her stomach began cramping with cold hunger as if she'd swallowed dozens of ice cubes, Cheryl made her way to *Necropolis*.

It was earlier than last night, the crowd thin.

Nightshade was nowhere in sight; she felt disappointed. She did, however, spot Poppy dancing with a large guy in ripped parachute pants and a chartreuse spiked half-Mohawk. The girl looked pale, but not much worse for wear.

Cheryl started across the floor, but before she could reach Poppy, Nightshade appeared between them.

Her body reacted like a plant moving toward the light. Every cell opened to receive him, and a wave of lust nearly knocked her off her feet. When he took her arm and led her outside, she went willingly.

"I was just going to see how Poppy's doing—"

He walked fast, pulling her up the street and into an alley. The pressure on her arm was beyond what was needed. "Don't be so rough." She jerked away. "What's with you? Last night you make love to me and now—"

"Make love? How pathetically romantic. I fucked you. We feed, we rut. A biological knee-jerk, that's all. Yours isn't exactly a warm body, but it was handy."

She avoided his eyes, feeling cut to the marrow, thrust into an alien landscape, alone, and not wanting to expose that. "You arrogant bastard! I'd rather dehydrate than put up with your coldness one more night."

"Easily arranged."

"Aleron was a saint compared to you. No wonder he left you!"

The arrow hit the target; he looked wounded for a second, before his features hardened. "I want the truth," he demanded.

"About what? I can't read your mind, remember?"

"What really happened to Saint Aleron?"

"I told you."

He moved on her, and she shouted, "Don't threaten me!" but that didn't stop him from grabbing her by the throat and pressing her up against the rough brick wall.

"There have been no serious fires in this city in the last month."

They glared at one another for long moments. Finally, he said, "You killed him, didn't you?"

"Yes," she whispered.

He let her go and, before she realized it, he had disappeared.

Cheryl searched the streets, *Necropolis*, Poppy's apartment. She broke into the theater. Nightshade was not there. She knew he likely wouldn't be back; it was no longer safe.

Standing in the middle of the vacant stage, sensing him everywhere and yet not here, her heart felt empty. Again. The pain of losing Aleron was compounded more than she could have imagined by the loss of Nightshade. In only one night he had fused with the deepest part of her and now, as with Aleron, she had been ripped in two. It was more than she could bear. Nightshade had warned her they were a solitary species. She should have paid attention, somehow locked her heart away. A sudden terror of eternity spread out before her and the long and lonely road she would walk. It sent her out into the streets again.

Eventually, she found him in the pool hall, dawn an hour away. She hadn't eaten and felt weak, and so stiff her joints would barely function.

He was the only one left in the room, shooting balls in the corner alone. She dragged a bar stool across the floor and sat nearby, but not too close. He didn't look at her or in any way acknowledge her presence until he paused and said, "'The weight of this sad time we must obey. Speak what we feel, not what we ought to say. The oldest hath borne most; we that are young, Shall never see so much, nor live so long.' *King Lear*. Do you know the tragedy?"

Nightshade racked the balls. He bent low over the table and broke the triangle, sinking three balls at once, each in a separate pocket. "Aleron taught me to play the game. We came here together for nearly five years after he changed me. I think he stayed with me the longest. I didn't bore him as much as the others. At first. But, in the end, he always grew bored. He would have gotten bored with you too, eventually."

"He did," Cheryl said shakily.

He paused again and then moved around the table. The blue two ball, the red three, the purple four. Each remaining ball in numerical sequence found a pocket. When he sank the brown and white striped fifteen, he racked them again.

"I killed him because I loved him too much." Her voice faltered more than she expected. She sighed heavily, feeling the weight of impending daylight pressing on her body and the dark emptiness descending into her soul. "I felt so sorry for him. He cried and cried; I didn't know what to do. He said he couldn't stand it any longer. Nothing engaged him. No one."

The memory of how Aleron had looked at her, his grey eyes pleading for something she could neither identify nor supply, struggling to find a reason in her and coming up empty.

"He had me chain him on top of the bed and leave the curtains open. I slept in the trunk. I didn't really understand. The next night, when I got up..." Her body trembled. "There was only ash and bits of bones."

Tears streamed down her face. "He told me you loved him more than all the others he'd changed. That's why he sent me to you. He said you'd understand somebody who could love. Who needed love." Her body spasmed.

The lights over the tables had become scalding, but she did not have the strength or the will to retreat to the cooler, darker shadows. Nightshade's eyes pulsed energy and strength and she wished she could draw some of it inside herself as she felt her own power ebbing.

She stood and walked away, unable to bear the ache of being near him. Maybe, if she could bring herself to face that ball of cleansing fire in the sky... Could there be salvation for the lost and lonely in annihilation?

A voice filled the room. "'Oh mistress mine, where are you roaming?'"

Cheryl wasn't aware of movement, but Nightshade was suddenly before her. He cupped her chin and lifted her wet face.

"You loved him most," he said. "You gave him what he longed for, what the rest of us couldn't give him. What I couldn't give him."

His sun-gold eyes seared away her loneliness. "You don't hate me?"

He kissed her lips tenderly then passionately. "Come home with me, vampire baby. I'll feed you and put you to bed. Tonight. Every night."

"*Take* me to bed," she corrected, throwing her arms around his neck.

He packed his cue into the case and, clinging to each other, they headed back to the theater.

Act II

Theatre of Cruelty

"I want the original script, no last-minute rewrites." Nightshade said.

He and Cheryl sat on the edge of the stage, dangling their feet like children, boot heels knocking the back boards, looking out at the nonexistent audience. Her aventurine eyes stared straight ahead, but her gaze was tuned to her private reality, as if waiting for an internal cue.

He caressed her chin for moments with his index finger, forcing her to face him. A copper chain holding a small copper ankh hung around her neck. She'd been wearing it the night she appeared at the pool hall two and a half weeks ago. Aleron's gift, no doubt. Nightshade restrained himself from ripping it from her throat.

He scanned her luscious features. They had fed early tonight; she no longer looked deflated, although her eyes held a haunted quality.

Her full lips invited him. He leaned in and licked them, smelling the blood they had consumed earlier.

Her lips parted the moment his tongue pressed for entrance. Her mouth tasted rich and meaty, the full flavor of blood remnants still lingering. He moved a hand behind her neck. For a split second she resisted, then yielded as he pulled her tight against him. He wanted to devour her. He wanted to fuck her.

Mind censored instinct, and he eased away.

Her eyes fire-danced. They beckoned him, and to keep his body from responding more than it already was to that heat, Nightshade hopped down into the orchestra pit and moved quickly through it and up into the theater. When he reached row 'Q' he took the aisle seat, orchestra center section.

The darkened house forced him to zero in on the bare, lit stage; a set would have been superfluous. She perched left of center as if an astute director with a sharp eye had carefully blocked this scene, placing her just so. Black backdrop, dark floor boards, red velvet swagged curtain. Female lead costumed in a long slate-leather skirt slit to the thigh, HarleyDavidson black jacket, black cowgirl boots with blood-red stitching.

Even from here she was one of the most beautiful creatures he'd ever seen. And, a natural on stage. The overhead lights accentuated the feminine contours of her face and body, but drew the audience of one right to her large, tormented eyes. He wondered what she had looked like before the change. Did her hair glow as if a spotlight shone on it constantly, the light radiating from her to illuminate an entire theater? Had her body swayed and undulated with the small, precise movements of a trained actor who conveys so much with so little? Did her gestures come as easily to her then as they did now, taunting both men and women, teasing, promising to open with only a slight twist of her lips or arch of her brow? He decided she must have been much the same, otherwise Aleron wouldn't have noticed her. Aleron only plundered the best.

Nightshade turned in the seat to cross his long legs in the aisle. He leaned back against the red velvet, arms folded over his chest, the crackling of his leather jacket the only sound.

He could tell when she was lying. The light her body emitted flickered the way a spotlight does when the electrical current becomes sporadic. He hoped she wouldn't lie to him now.

He wanted to trust her. He needed her more than she could understand. His existence had become repetitive, a one-man eternal touring company, seven nights a week in a show that had long ago bombed. He'd been waiting for some new direction, a way to alter what felt like an endless performance before an audience too unsophisticated to appreciate his abilities. He needed someone to play off. A connection. He and Cheryl were so close to forming one. A part like this was rare, and he was afraid he might blow it.

"Tell me about Aleron," he said gently.

She held her breath. Stage fright. She had forgotten her lines, or didn't know how to deliver them. Rehearsal was over; it was too late to run and hide.

Suddenly, she sighed. Her shoulders slumped from the pressure of being held rigid, and her jaw relaxed a bit, making her face less masklike. "He'd been watching me," she said. "For a long time. I didn't know."

"Where did you meet him?"

"In, well, a kind of church. *Freewill* is different, though. It's New Age. Sort of a community. They're into wholeness, getting in touch with your helpers, with a higher power—"

"Ah, Janice."

"You know her?"

"She's one of us."

Cheryl looked startled. She caught the corner of her lower lip between her teeth and nodded. "I'd only gone there once before. I had no idea Aleron was even there. It's as if he was invisible or something. He was good at disguising himself."

Nightshade thought about the night he'd met Aleron. That chameleon quality struck him right away. Aleron could be whoever and whatever he wanted to be, or what you wanted him to be. Lover. Protector. Persecutor. But, never your victim.

"...and that night, as I was walking to the bus stop in the rain, he drove up in a silver Fiat, the windows tinted like mirrors. He rolled down a window and said, "'You left *Freewill* behind. Come in out of the cold. I can take you where you want to go.'

"I remember bending to look through the passenger's window at him. Inside the car it was like a black hole, with only these grey eyes. They were the center of the universe, and I felt dragged towards them as if everything...as if *I* was compelled to revolve around them. I don't know what made me get in.

"I felt shivery and said, 'Can you turn up the heat?'

"'I will.' His voice was a promise.

"He kept staring at me, and again, the omniscient power of those eyes hit me. You'll think I'm nuts, but it's as if they were made of grey glass. I mean, I could see right *through* them. Inside, I glimpsed snatches of a flat alien landscape, fascinating and horrifying. He made me so nervous I started babbling, something like, 'So, do you go to the *Freewill* often? I've been there twice. It's an interesting place—'

"'Cheryl, I will visit your locked vaults and stroke the darkest contours of your soul.'

"I froze. What he said was so weird, so poetic, so... but, put so matter of factly. *Just another hustle*, I told myself. But, there was an undercurrent of demand or command or...I don't know what. Instead of telling him to go fuck himself, or laughing it off, I blurted out, 'How do you know my name?'

"'Do not fear me. Destiny pulses and throbs with a tantalizing rhythm all its own. The most a mere mortal can do is adjust the volume. If destiny decides to play you as a passion song, you'd best dance to that melody of your own volition, sweet Cheryl, because whether or not you want to, you have drawn a partner, and you will be dancing.'

"'Listen, I think you'd better let me out—'

"He switched on the CD player. Haunting sounds burst through the car's interior from half a dozen speakers. The eerie *a cappella* music felt like an attack, violating every orifice of my body. I clamped my hands over my ears, and practically curled into a ball, but the women's cries pricked at my pores like tiny insects determined to dig their way inside me. Within seconds, every thought in my head had been annihilated. My body vibrated from note to note and became the chanting. I felt I didn't exist apart from those sounds. I became a cloud, formed, dissolved and reformed by fate, completely bound up with the fundamental essence of the universe.

"Suddenly, the sound died. It was so abrupt, I screamed. Silence crushed my eardrums. My clothes were soaked with sweat. My body trembled, out of my control, assaulted in a different way because now that the music had stopped, I felt...empty.

"'Hildegard von Bingen, born in 1098,' he said. 'Abbess of a community of nuns attached to a Benedictine monastery; composer of contained ecstasy. Penetration by a Gregorian chant is not much different than being penetrated by a god. Have you not secretly wished to be impaled by a god?'

"He pushed the steering wheel up, then slid over the gear shift, moving as smoothly as a snake. Before I could protest, he was on top of me and my seat was completely back. The car had stopped; nothing looked familiar. Only his grey eyes. When I looked into them, I felt comforted and disturbed at the same time.

"But, the darkness surrounding me was absorbing me. I was terrified, but stunned. And when his grey eyes stared so intently into mine, all I could do was surrender to their transparent brilliance because they had become the only thing in the universe I could cling onto to keep from disappearing.

"'Feel how deeply I enter you,' he whispered. 'Learn and remember. You will pierce me as deeply, to my core. I've waited a long time for your light to burn through my darkness.'

"The strange chanting returned, capturing me, ravishing me, leaving my naked body limp in his arms.

"His penis pressed hard against me, insistent. My thighs were slick with juices and parted as if I couldn't control them, but I didn't want to control anything. He thrust into me once, fast and deep. That movement was so serious and passionate. Fierce. My head fell back. I sobbed when his icy lips clamped onto my throat. Despite the chilly air that made me shiver, my blood boiled through my veins. That scorching heat ripped through me like a forest fire, consuming me as it ate my genitals.

"My hips bucked and writhed under his hard thrusts. The music took me up, and his determined body dragged me back down to earth again. He controlled me completely. I felt caught in the jaws of pain and pleasure. My brain stopped sending messages, abandoning my body and soul to this delirious ride on the edge of time and space. Exquisite explosions rocked me, one after the other, and they went on forever. I heard myself screaming in agony and ecstasy, wanting him to stop, to never stop. And all the while, I knew the life was being sucked from my body and my soul was becoming chained to his. And, I didn't care."

Nightshade was aware of a knot of tension in his shoulders, and rotated his neck. Her elaborately told tale was too similar to his own. The seduction, the compulsion to give himself over to Aleron, a compulsion that soon turned into an obsession.

She was staring down at her folded hands.

"There's one line missing in that scene," he said.

Cheryl looked up. Even from a distance her eyes were redrimmed. Bloodtinged tears stained her cheeks. She shook her head slightly.

"I want to hear the words."

She still hesitated. If Aleron were here now, she'd be at his feet. Her voice sounded weak and needy. "I loved him."

"Yes." Nightshade nodded.

Her body quivered. He wanted to go to her, comfort her, make love to her, drink from her and let her drink from him. But, none of it would matter. Even dead, Aleron was a wedge between them, maybe even more so than if he were still alive, or whatever this state he had brought them into could be called. And, he not only kept them from one another, he kept them from themselves.

She began to climb down off the stage.

"Stay there!" he shouted.

She looked afraid. Lonely. Now was not the time to comfort her; he had to keep reminding himself of that or he would do something stupid, and Aleron would win. "The rest."

She leaned back against the edge of the stage. "I woke in a strange bed. It was the next night, I think. My head felt empty, and my body hollow. Everything sounded so loud, and I heard so many noises, all mixed together. I saw light through my eyelids. Shadows. I didn't want to move.

"Aleron's voice seemed to be sliding around inside my head. 'Open your eyes, beloved.'

"I must have opened them, because his face was there, the long white hair framing his angelic features, those sparkling grey eyes that beckoned to other worlds, wonderful places of passion and despair. He looked like a proud father, eyeing his offspring for the first time. Delight. Wonder. Boredom.

"When I saw that, it hurt. I didn't know why he looked bored, and I was afraid to ask, but I felt inadequate in some basic way. Do you know what I'm talking about?"

"Yes." Nightshade remembered the look and knew the feeling of self doubt intimately.

"He fed me right away, and only when my limbs came alive, and I began to breathe again, did it hit me that I hadn't been feeling anything at all. That night, I was completely out of it."

"How did he feed you?"

Suddenly, she shoved away from the stage and stormed up the aisle. "You don't have any fucking right to know that!"

He was out of his seat and on her before she could defend herself. "Don't tell me what rights I have! You wouldn't be here if it wasn't for my generosity."

"I owe you for eternity? Just tell me how to pay you back, so we can even it, okay?"

"You can even it by telling me what I need to know. Give me the truth for a change!"

She looked caught for a second. Her arm swung out to slap him, but he snagged her wrist. He grabbed her hair and pulled her head back, exposing her throat. He felt ferocious, and made sure to let her see his teeth and his fury.

"You're not my equal yet, honey." He wasn't about to put up with these remnants of mortal embarrassment and guilt. Too much was at stake.

Cheryl backed down, an animal resigned to the other's dominance; this battle cannot be won. The blaze in her eyes dimmed as her body took on a submissive posture.

He let her go, but turned away. If she was going to attack, now was the time. He had turned his back on her to test her. Did she feel any loyalty to him? If she didn't, he'd better know about it before it was too late.

Cheryl didn't attack. Instead, she took a seat across the aisle from his. Now that they both sat and faced each other, she stared directly at him. Hatred flared in her eyes from this safer distance. If loyalty existed behind the enmity, he couldn't see it.

"Mostly, I took it from his cock. Every night he fed me and then he fucked me. Happy? Or do you want the details of that too?"

Those icy words chilled the air between them.

"You enjoyed yourself, I presume."

"Yes. Of course. Didn't you enjoy getting fucked by Aleron?"

Colder. Her attack wasn't going to be physical, but it was as sharp as her claws. "The plot's slowing down, honey. Act Two. Move it along."

"There's nothing more to say. I fed, I fucked. It was fun."

"And, when did it stop being fun?"

"It never stopped."

"Then, cut to Act Three."

"What do you want to know?"

"The climax."

"I was with him ten days. When we weren't eating or screwing, I was listening. He talked about love. And despair. And alchemy. He was an alchemist, you know."

Nightshade felt his jaw clench, which fortunately kept his mouth shut. He knew. All of that. And, far more than she did.

"He showed me this chemical experiment. He heated cinnabar in a kind of tall copper pot he called an athanor. Then, he added something—potassium metal, I think he said, but I'm not sure—and it became a solid. And then he put that in water, and it began to steam, and flames shot up. And, quicksilver fell out. It was magical! He was trying to show me how the universe works. Nothing is ever lost, it just changes form. He said our state is like this too. We aren't dead in the usual sense, what most people think of as death. We're just in a different form. We appear to be solid, but it depends what ingredients you add."

Nightshade let a sound of disgust erupt, which didn't dampen her soliloquy.

"One night—the only night he took me out of the apartment—he showed me how he could disappear. We went to an old cemetery, the one across town, where that famous poet's buried? It was a beautiful night, clear sky, a moon so full we had plenty of light to read the inscriptions as we strolled among the crypts and simple graves. Aleron stopped at a gorgeous mausoleum, built of grey marble, with a stone Gabriel sitting on the peaked roof, and the faces of two cherubs on either side of the door.

"'Walk back towards the path, ten paces,' he told me. 'Say my name, and then turn around.'

"I did. When I turned, Aleron was gone. I searched the cemetery and called him for half an hour, more frantic every second. Suddenly, I came around to the front of the mausoleum again and there he was, leaning against the doorway between the cherubs, smiling, just like when I last saw him.

"'Where did you go?'

"'It is you who disappeared, beloved. I have been here all along.'

"He swore to me he hadn't moved. And, when I stepped back a dozen feet and looked—the way he told me to look, not with my eyes but with my imagination, expecting him *not* to be there—suddenly, I saw how he blended with the shadows, the way his body moulded to the pillars and how the grey marble doorway camouflaged him. His form subtly shifted and fused. The silence made him completely disappear, at least to my eyes. He had become part of the structure, and I couldn't see him at all."

"Theatrical tricks."

Her head jerked up, back to the reality of the theater, the reality of him. She shook her head. "No. Not a trick."

He jumped to his feet and paced the ramp-like aisle with long strides, struggling unsuccessfully to keep his fury in check.

"Don't be so naive! Do you think you're the first bitch he charmed with that illusion? Aleron the Great Magician. The Metamorphose! Come and see the creature with the supernatural powers of a deity! Watch him turn his body into blood, and the blood into wine for your consumption, just like Christ!"

His voice echoed through the empty theater for a second until her words slashed the air. "You saw that, didn't you? And more. And, you're jealous. He's what you're not. Great."

He moved faster than her eye could track. She jumped to her feet and turned, startled, staring up at him behind her.

"Yes," he said, "I watched the Great Master of Mirage take his best shots, and learned at his hallowed feet. But, you were just getting to the good part. How you charred him. Don't skimp on the details."

"Why are you being so cruel? You say you once loved him—"

"Because this Theater of the Absurd has dragged on long enough to bore me. Intermission's over. Time for the final curtain."

They both sat and glared at one another. Waiting.

She gripped the arm of the seat hard. Her knuckles turned white. Her face had become a plaster mask. A Greek tragedy was underway here and he didn't like the tone. “Don’t break the furniture,” he said lightly.

She looked down, then up. All he could offer her was a strained smile. It was enough, apparently; her face softened, and that perpetual hunger, for him, for blood returned. She wanted him inside her. His cock. The blood cruising his veins. But more, she wanted Aleron, and he knew that. It gave him the hard edge he needed to push her. “Get to it if you want any kind of snack before bed.”

Hope filled her face. He wasn’t delusional enough to believe it all focused on him, but he would take what he could from her. All that Aleron had left.

“He liked to tie me up with thin copper chains, binding me to the bed, to the doorframe, anywhere, my body naked, and pried open. I guess those chains wouldn’t hold me now, but then, I was so weak. And hungry. All the time. ‘Understand that I possess you,’ he said, every night, all night long. It was like chanting, the words eating into my brain until every cell of my body knew it was true. ‘I possess you, I possess you.’ I did belong to him.

“I watched him like a puppy watches its master, each time he moved, a slight gesture, even when he wasn’t moving, just staring out the window as if waiting for something. I was desperate for attention. I existed in a state of perpetual hunger. Throughout the night he fed me drops of blood, randomly, whetting my appetite. It was never enough. I was always hungry, wanting. Sometimes he talked, about the others, about you, and that terrified me. He was beyond misery. He said no one was left, and he had no way to get high. He’d done it all, many times over. I tried, but my words didn't affect him. Instead, his depression sucked me down with him until at times I thought I'd smother under the despair. My heart turned to lead in my chest and I didn't even have the energy to breathe. And then, suddenly, he would be playing with my body, bringing me close to orgasm, sucking and biting my nipples until I was screaming for release, licking my clitoris, entering me, anywhere, everywhere. And always he stopped short. My body writhed and throbbed. I've never been so excited. There were moments when I felt, if he just looks at me I'll come. But, of course, those were the moments when he wouldn't look my way at all, or he would leave the apartment and I'd be alone with desires that nearly drove me insane. I spent a lot of time crying. But, my tears didn't move him. Neither did my anger. All I know is that the cycle continued. Endlessly. The feeding. The silence. His despair. The wild sex. And, throughout it all, the words: 'I possess you,' over and over. I've never felt so completely and deliciously helpless, so overwhelmed with passion. Can you understand that?"

He couldn't answer.

"Aleron became my every thought. Anything he asked, I would have done for him. I know he knew that. When he told me to open the curtains and chain him to the bed and sleep in the trunk, I did that, without thinking about what he was asking, never considering the sunlight, trusting him like a child. Hoping he would reward me for being obedient."

Her shoulders fell forward and shook as she sobbed.

"I didn't know. I didn't let myself know."

Nightshade moved across the aisle. He crouched down and took her fragile shoulders in his hands. "Stop it, Cheryl! Trust me, he's not worth crying over. Tell me the rest. Quickly."

"Why?" Her face was a mask of agony. An agony he felt too sharply. Seeing it smeared across her features steeled him.

"You can cry for him for the rest of eternity, but right now you'll tell me what I want to know!"

The stern tone sliced into her. He knew it would be hard for her to forgive him for what she perceived as callousness, but he had no choice. They could huddle here together in a pool of self-pity and endless longing, or he could do what needed to be done.

She pulled back, shaking free. Her moist eyes hardened into cool emeralds, flashing a barely restrained hatred. "The end? It's simple. I got out of the trunk to find a bed full of ash and bone slivers in the shape of my lover."

"What else?"

Her lips pressed hard together, as though she might not tell him. Suddenly, it was as though she realized this particular scene wasn't worth fighting over. "I found a letter. In his jacket pocket."

"Saying?"

"Saying what I should do. Gather his remains up in the sheet. Bury them. Come to you."

"Where did you bury them?"

"Why do you want to know?"

"He's dead. Why do you care?"

"Because I loved him. You didn't. That's obvious. Whatever happened between you and Aleron wasn't love from your end. You just want to get even because he stopped loving you. I can see that now."

"You don't see anything. He's got you mesmerized from the grave. He seduced hundreds over the centuries. You think what you feel is love. It's bondage, and those pretty copper chains you romanticize about were just the most obvious part of the package. It's getting late. And, I'm tired of this tragedy. I want to know where you buried the remains of the great metaphysician."

"I'm not going to tell you."

"Don't even think that, because you *are* going to tell me!"

She shook her head. "You can hurt me, I know you can, but I won't betray Aleron."

Time was running out. It was a big risk but he had to do something. "I'm not going to hurt you, Cheryl, not in the way you think. But, I will deprive you of blood. And, since you seem to love being chained up, I can do that too, and lick your cunt just the way Aleron did, so you can get off while you're starving."

"Bastard!" She flew at him, her nails sharpened talons, slashing into the flesh of his cheeks, her jaws snapping towards his throat.

They struggled briefly before he brought her down. His weight pressed her facefirst to the carpet until she was gnawing at the fibers. He held her wrists behind her neck, and his body weight kept her pinned. In time they would be more equal, but for the moment he still had the edge. "Spare yourself a few grams of agony. Tell me where I can find the remains of the recently departed."

"No! He's mine! I love him! You never did!"

He let her sob and scream and curse him. But, eventually, all the crying and bucking against his body as she tried to throw him off stopped. As she lay under him, her breathing returning to normal, he patted her hair, a simple act of comfort; he felt the will seep out of her like a spirit drifting away from the earth.

"What are you going to do?" she asked in a small, frightened voice.

"Finish the script."

"What does that mean? I told you he's dead."

"Where did you bury him?"

"Why can't you trust me? I've given you everything else, why isn't that enough? Why do you always stay hidden from me?"

"Because, you still love him."

"I love you."

"Not the way you love him."

"Aleron's dead. Can't you let him rest in peace?"

"Peace? For who? You? Me? Don't try to make me into him, Cheryl. If you care about us—"

"No, if *you* care about us. And I wonder just how much you do care."

"Meaning?"

"You'll destroy us. What we have now, what we can

have together. Why can't you let it be?"

She pushed back and he let her up. They sat on the floor cross-legged, facing each other, the tension thick as an invisible wall that threatened to become visible. "I didn't know I could love you," she said softly, "as much as I loved him. But, what you're asking is destroying that love. I guess it comes down to a choice: You can have me, or you can have Aleron's ashes to desecrate. If you care about me at all, you'll forget about him."

He didn't even pause. "Where are the ashes?"

She looked as if he'd slapped her. Then, her face turned stony. She got to her feet and glared down at him. "The cemetery across town. The mausoleum I told you about."

She hurried down the aisle and up onto the stage. Her boot heels clacked hard against the floorboards as she crossed to the back. Just before she exited, she turned. Light danced off her perfect cheekbones. Those large green eyes had narrowed and turned to hard jade. "I won't be back, you know."

She turned and he heard the stage door open and then slam shut.

He brought his hands together and clapped them three times slowly, despairingly. "Bravo. Encore." But she didn't return. And he didn't go after her.

Act III

Metadrama

Under the unearthly glow of a bloated moon, Cheryl watched Nightshade's shadowy form slip between the gravestones. He treated the three low steps leading to the silent tomb as one, but stopped at the grey marble door with Gabriel poised for flight above his head. He seemed to be procrastinating, or maybe steeling himself to enter. His hands reached out crucifixion style, and grasped the two stark cherub faces. Suddenly, he snapped his head to the left and stared straight in her direction.

Cheryl ducked back behind the large oak, but not in time.

"Coming in for the show, or do you just want to catch the sound effects?"

Resigned, she stepped into the moonlight.

She hated herself for being here, for spying on Nightshade—especially after what happened at the theater tonight—for trying to protect Aleron's memory, a memory that, the more she thought about it, the more she realized how tainted it was with somcthing dark and unpleasant she didn't want to look at. But, she was here. She might as well see it all.

His eyes were intense from stress as he turned to watch her. She noticed his hands balled into fists at his sides. His jaw was tight.

When she got close enough, it became obvious he'd fed, and a lot, on the way here. White moonbeams brought out the contrasts in his flushed skin. His full lips were darker than she'd ever seen them, and those sun-gold eyes sharply piercing.

He grabbed the padlock she had affixed to the door—as Aleron's note had instructed—and yanked it from the clasp. He shoved the marble door inward and then disappeared into the darkness.

She followed on his heels. The cool interior of the mausoleum, the odor of decaying earth, the utter silence, all brought home what had happened so recently. She felt claustrophobic, and wanted to run from this house of the dead. She should be dead, or was she dead?...she didn't remember dying. And yet, it now seemed as though she would never die. Maybe that very knowledge made this place both attractive and repulsive. And then there was what remained of Aleron.

Small slatted windows—air vents, really—let in moonlight. The stone coffin took up most of the space. Aleron had anticipated his own demise, apparently—the crypt, the coffin. That had unnerved her. When she brought his remains here, the lid, carved with his effigy, was already pushed aside at the top corner. A small triangle lay open, just enough to allow the sheet containing the ashes and slivers of bone to be surrendered to their permanent home. It took all her strength to shift that corner of the lid the twelve inches needed to seal up the casket for what she thought at the time would be forever.

Now, she was back here, with Nightshade. She didn't know exactly what he had in mind, but she knew it would be a violation of some kind, and that she could not bear.

"Please," she begged. "Let's go away. Get a fresh start..."

The two copper chains Aleron's letter had instructed her to secure around the coffin were still there. Nightshade ripped both apart as if they were made of paper. He shoved the lid hard. Stone scraped stone as the lid plunged over the edge of the sarcophagus and crashed to the concrete floor, breaking into half a dozen large chunks, clouding the air with dust.

"'Alas, poor Yorick,...' Nobody knew you well, babe."

Cheryl noticed for the first time that the interior of the coffin was copper-lined, like the copper chains Aleron had bound her with, the athanor. She fingered the ankh around her neck.

Carefully, Nightshade's slender fingers untied the black sheet and spread it open. Even most of Aleron's bones had burned to ash, making her wonder the night she'd found him if he had been conscious as his body dissolved. To preserve her own sanity, she'd decided he couldn't have been. Now, he was a pile of physical fragments, as grey as his eyes had been, but lustreless by comparison.

Her body trembled. She could hardly breathe. Something awful was about to happen.

She stepped towards Nightshade. "Please. I'm begging you. You don't—"

His head jerked in her direction. The look on his face silenced her fast. It was as though she'd never seen him before. He was hard, unbending. Obsessed. Her body began to spasm. She had never seen anything like what stood before her now.

He must have caught his reflection in her eyes. "Come here," he said softly, pulling her close. "Trust me!"

She wanted to. She needed to. "But, what—"

His mouth captured hers, pulling, twisting, sucking on her lips hungrily, prying them apart so that his tongue could enter. She tasted blood and her brain shut down. His hands, frantic, rode her body, and their heat made her as desperate as he was.

She tore at his pants. As her fingers stroked his swollen flesh, he turned her around and bent her forward. The space between the coffin and the wall behind was narrow; he made her lean all the way across the casket. She gripped the far edge of the icy stone.

He picked up one of the copper chains and wrapped it around her waist, twice, then around his own. It was a symbolic gesture; chains wouldn't hold her now, at least she didn't think so. The hand holding the chain gathered her skirt at the slit and pulled the fabric back and up. His other hand slid between her legs and tore away the crotch of her panties. She gasped and he pulled the chain taut.

She stared at the ashes two feet from her face as Nightshade entered her. He slid in deep, and she moaned. Her long hair hung down and brushed Aleron's remains. The burning walls inside her wept as they compressed. Nightshade's thrusts created ripples of charged energy. Small eruptions shot sparks through her body that returned to her vagina in the span of a breath. Within seconds, she clutched the edge of the coffin violently. Stone crumbled in her hands. She arched her back and screamed when the inferno exploded.

He was still inside her, still firm. In a second, when she recovered a bit, she would give him pleasure, any way he wanted it. But for another moment, while she found her way back to ground zero,...

His hands slid down her forearms and locked onto her wrists. He brought her arms up and crossed them over her chest, and then pulling her back upright. Her head fell against his shoulder. He lifted her right wrist to his mouth and she sighed, anticipating the dark kiss. Instead, pain seared her.

His long teeth sliced too deep into her left wrist, at an angle, tearing things that shouldn't be torn. Quickly, he pierced his own wrist.

"What are you doing?" she asked, nervous. When he didn't answer, she began to struggle. "Let me go!" But, he'd fed so much, and recently, he was far stronger. He bit into the artery of her right wrist, and his own. Then, he forced her over the coffin again.

"Stop! Don't take my blood!" she screamed. "I don't

have enough!" Blood jerked out of her body, spurting from the severed arteries, gushing from veins onto the ashes below. With each crimson jet stream, she weakened. As her energy dimmed, so did her ability to fight him.

Nightshade was a rock she could not move. She shrieked and ranted, kicking, twisting, and finally crying bloody tears of fear and frustration until she could no longer hold her head up. Within fragments of a minute most of the blood had left her, wasted over a pile of mouldering ash. The wounds in her wrists lay open, but nothing much was coming out. She felt empty, and on the edge of collapsing.

He held her there until all the blood from his own body had saturated the remains. If he felt as depleted as she, Cheryl had no idea where he found the strength to pull her up and keep both of them vertical.

Her mind flowed down a dark river, melding with the current, diluted by the expanding black liquid to become every sea in the world.

She could not see clearly, or hear. And when the wet copper scent tapped her olfactory nerve, at first it was unidentifiable. Her eyelids cracked open to blurry vision. No, it was not her eyesight!

Smoke swelled from the coffin, and Cheryl watched transfixed. It was as if the cold blood had splattered onto a hot grill. Sizzling. Acrid vapours billowed into the air, clouding the room, enveloping them in a dense haze.

The air grew glacial, laced with the stench of putrefaction. The building rumbled beneath her feet. Her teeth chattered uncontrollably while her limbs went numb.

A low snarl turned her nerves to ice water. Something dark undulated up through the fog, and took on a spectral shape. Two dead grey circles with fiery centers pierced the gloom.

As if a preternatural wind blew through the crypt, the mist cleared.

Three beings now inhabited the marble chamber.

Aleron's ashen eyes aligned like magnets, attracted to the iron in the dried blood on her arms, on Nightshade's raw wounds.

His mouth clamped onto Nightshade's wrist, sucking, a white tongue lashing out. When he'd gotten all that was possible, the seated skeleton glared at her. Rice paper flesh stretched over bone. Nearly hairless, scarred, bloody lips bent on siphoning from her what she no longer had burned her skin like dry ice.

His eyes began to sparkle, tinted window panes when the sun hits. It reminded her of the first time she saw them, when they had been all that existed for her. But now, his face resembled a hideous serpent-like gargoyle, alive with madness. She could not stand to look at such distortion, but she could not turn away.

Her body felt heavy, her head light. She sobbed from the pain of being bled dry. She tried, but couldn't pull her wrist away from his mouth. Aleron didn't seem to notice her struggle, but Nightshade did. He yanked her backwards, hard. Aleron's mouth came away with a loud pop as the suction broke.

Those eyes swirled in demented brilliance. She was drawn towards them and what lay beyond. But he was feral, ravenous; he would have gone after her for more if she'd had any more. Before she realized it, his icy hands reached under her T-shirt and caressed her breasts, chilling her, thrilling her. She leaned back against Nightshade. Cold seeped through her pores, tightening her nipples, freezing what little energy she had left, but she could not stop him.

Aleron ran a hand over Nightshade's gaunt face, down his chest, down to his crotch, his steely pinprick eyes never leaving the faded suns. "Phenomenal. To die the true death and return. No experience compares. Agony equals transformation. I am truly a god. *Your* god.

"And you both, my creations—so vulnerable now. And, I am famished. You should have brought more; I told you I would need more."

"You...you knew you were coming back?" Cheryl gasped, astonished.

Nightshade pushed away the hand fondling his cock and zipped his pants. His breathing sounded shallow and she saw his eyes flicker, as if their light might go out. "You got the starring role in this vehicle," he said to Aleron. "I played my part. What more do you want?"

Cheryl broke away from both of them. She staggered to the foot of the coffin, holding onto the stone; the chain around her waist loosened. "I don't get it."

"Nightshade vowed an oath many decades ago. Should

he learn of my demise, he was compelled to revive me at the next full moon. Following my instructions, of course."

Awareness dawned on her. "You died so you could come back! And sent me to Nightshade because you knew he'd bring you back." Confusion gripped her again. "Why would you do that?" But she was afraid she knew the answer.

"And, why not?" As he climbed out of the coffin, his eyes left hers and moved to Nightshade's. His rictus grin bared enormous eye teeth, stained scarlet. "My theory proved correct."

"Then, this production has finished its run," Nightshade said.

"Has it?"

Cheryl held onto the coffin with both hands. She had to. "You used me," she said in a small voice. "Both of you."

Aleron stroked her cheek absently as he continued to look at Nightshade, shaking his head in confusion, as though he had no idea what she was talking about. Nightshade only stared at him.

But it was clear to her now. Aleron had put her through agony, just so he could get off big time. And, Nightshade had helped him. At her expense.

Nightshade let the cool stones of the wall prop him up. He studied the slim naked form, severely scarred from the flames that had devoured him. Those scars would fade, in time. That was too bad. Aleron wouldn't have anything physical to remind him, and his memory had become a labyrinth of crumbling medieval script fragments, the lines of which he had a habit of misquoting.

Nightshade had his own scars, emotional in nature. But now, they seemed to be nothing more than a midsummer night's dream. Yet, he had always remembered his dreams vividly, and his nightmares.

His term of indenture was over. For the first time in his immortal existence, he was a free agent. Aleron had bled to create him. He had given his blood to recreate Aleron. Nightshade felt the moment the bond snapped. The set had been cleared, and only the actors were left. Predictably, Aleron didn't seem to notice the change, or at least he didn't let on.

"The pain of death is as nothing to the pain of rebirth," Aleron said, pontificating as usual. "Dissolution is harsh, but predictable and follows a course in keeping with what we already understand. But, to be reformed...I did not know what I would become, but knew I would become greater than I had been. Never less. Of course, I could not be less than I am."

Aleron was a user, incapable of love. Did he feel any emotions, or had they all shrivelled centuries ago? Too many nights Nightshade had lain in the darkness, terrified he might one day become Aleron: jaded, hopeless. His need escalating. Desperate for something or someone to fill his existence with meaning, if only for moments here and there.

"I glimpsed neither Jehovah nor Lucifer. I hovered in a chrysalis between life and death, simply waiting for a sign of the alteration to occur. It is a state much like sleep, but with more conscious awareness. Those such as yourselves would not easily tolerate this state. I, however, am a more than sentient being, and my will made the difference."

More insults. Low shots. Subtle, like a chilly gust. Aleron had to be on top. Always. Knocking him off that self-perpetuating pedestal would be sheer pleasure.

Cheryl stood motionless, looking confused. Angry. Not quite able to believe what was happening. Aleron flirted with her, curling her hair around his fingers, tongue-kissing her palm, easing in close, as if she should forget that he had used her. A seductive smile played across his lips. He was so handsome. Irresistible. Despite how distorted his body was, those classical features, now framed only by wisps of white hair, were remarkable. His grey eyes arrested both mortals and immortals alike. Nightshade remembered staring at that face and that body for what had seemed like an eternity and never tiring of the sight. Aleron's looks were his blessing and his curse. He'd never had to work at immortality. There had been few challenges. Now, there were none.

Aleron fingered the ankh lying in the hollow of her throat. "Copper, a feminine metal, the symbol of Venus and Frida, the conductor of life and death. You understand, only through your being may we gods move with ease. I am truly immortal now. Nightshade is in error, as I told him many times. And, I have proven this to you both. I sailed the river Styx and have returned to confirm what I knew before I first embarked on this alchemical journey:

there is no purpose to existence."

Like a character too ignorant to realize he's destined to be written out of a script, Aleron kept up the charming discourse. But, he was not talking with them, or even to them. He'd never been inclusive, except to further his purposes. And yet, some part of him must know that the theater was closing, the company disbanding.

He glided around the crowded space gracefully, theatrically, his style unique, admirable. He stared at Cheryl, but spoke to Nightshade. "Such submissiveness. A perfect container. A true enchantress. We three belong together. You will you look after her until my return."

Abdicating his responsibility. As always. He didn't want either of them, but it was not his way to say so. And, he wouldn't admit even to himself that they were no longer his possessions.

Nightshade wanted to hate Aleron, but hate was no longer an option. He pitied this one who had survived centuries, enduring an anguish so great, he couldn't even admit it to himself. Aleron had never been able to handle truth. And, the truth had become monstrous: he had reached the end of his time. There were no more plots to twist. No new plays would be written in limbo.

Cheryl was about to confront him. Nightshade moved up behind her. His fingers on the back of her neck sent a message. As if his thought planted itself in her head, her mouth closed.

"I'll take care of her."

Aleron glanced outside. His role was not an enviable one: warrior crazed from too many battles. He didn't realize that he'd lost the war. He paraded the battlefield like a hero, when in fact he was a figure of scorn.

He leaned in. His lips brushed Cheryl's, then Nightshade's. Behind the transparent windows of his eyes, a shadowy being fled the stage. They would not meet again.

Before Aleron could sense that, he moved out into the ivory light painting the sky. He did not turn when he asked in a quiet voice, "What it is you used to love to quote me? Concerning reliance."

"'I have always relied on the kindness of strangers.'"

Aleron paused only a heartbeat, and then moved briskly down the steps and across the graveyard through the morning mist. When the air thinned, he was gone.

"Why did you do it?" Cheryl demanded. Her eyes flashed fury. "You could have brought him back yourself. Why drag me into this?"

"Isn't it obvious?" He took the copper ankh in his hand and suddenly ripped the chain from her throat. He threw Aleron's *gift* outside.

The impact of that action hit home, but she couldn't restrain herself. "But he fucked both of us over, and you let him get away with it!"

Aleron had wounded her. Nightshade hoped he could repair the damage.

"You had the chance," she went on. "Why didn't you tell him to—?"

His finger touched her lips. "'Swift as a shadow, short as

any dream, Brief as the lightning in the collied night, That, in a spleen, unfolds both heaven and earth, And ere a man hath power to say, Behold! The jaws of darkness do devour it up: So quick bright things come to confusion.'"

Her eyes flickered, and then softened as understanding seeped in. "You could have crushed him, but you didn't." She exhaled, as if she'd been holding her breath for a very long time. "I guess it's you who loved him most."

Suddenly, pain flashed across her pale face. "I'm so hungry."

"I know. So am I. But the sun will be up any minute. There's no time to find food, or get back to the theater. We can stay here. Barricade the door, use the coffin to block the light. We'll be safe. If you want to stay with me, that is."

She hesitated. Her green eyes were clear, but did she know she had a choice? Him. Aleron. Neither of them. It was the last he worried most about.

"Do you want me to stay?" she asked.

"'Doubt thou the stars are fire; Doubt that the sun doth move; Doubt truth to be a liar; But never doubt I love.'"

Her arms circled his neck. He pulled her close and kissed her lips longingly, lovingly. She was a feather in his arms, but her essence filled his heart.

They blocked the door from the inside, nestling in safety, until daylight once more gave way to the world of darkness.

⌖

Note to Readers

Dearest Reader,

Thank you for reading my novella. I hope you enjoyed the story. Writers need reviews and if you would take a minute to review *Vampyre Theatre* I'd be most appreciative.

And, I have a few suggestions for you!

- First:
The band *Vampire Beach Babes* has recorded a song that was inspired by *Vampyre Theatre*. Just copy the url into your browser and can listen to Snake free here:
https://tinyurl.com/vxz59sr

- Second:
A graphic novel of these stories exists. *The Vampyre's Theater* is published by PreForce Publishing, and if you like graphics, keep an eye out for it.

- Check out another of my vampire novellas *Wild Hunt*, in eBook, and also in print from Baskerville Books.

- Lastly:
If you enjoy my work, please look for my newest vampire novel series (excerpt below). There are six titles, available in eBook and print everywhere.

Thrones of Blood series

Vol 1 - Revenge of the Vampir King
Vol 2 - Sacrifice of the Hybrid Princess
Vol 3 - Abduction of Two Rulers **(Excerpt below)**
Vol 4 - Savagery of the Rebel King
Vol 5 - Anguish of the Sapiens Queen
Vol 6 - Imperilment of the Hybrids (available 2020)

Excerpt

Abduction of Two Rulers

Book 3 in the THRONES OF BLOOD series

Chapter One

"Death is the only God that loves not bribes..."
Aristophanes

"A gift for you, traitor! Choke on the blue!"

When the cell door opened, Thanatos jumped at it, but the three vampirii were quick and strong and he was weak—they hadn't been starved as he had been.

Powerful pale vampiric arms repelled him across the small cell and at the same time, shoved a body through the opening. Instantly, the steel-enforced door was slammed closed and as Thanatos rammed it, locked from the outside. He heard cold laughter and the words, "There won't be much left when he's done."

In a split second he turned on the body, not caring if it was human or animal, male or female, not seeing features or fur, clothing or flesh, only hearing the pounding of a beating heart. Blood aroma beneath the skin wafted through pores. The scent he inhaled tuned visual and tactile, his reaction visceral. The blood lured him like a siren that he had no hope of resisting but had to possess.

He was on the mortal, ripping fabric from the throat, sinking teeth into the neck, through skin and muscle, past connective tissue and deep into the vein in a fragmented second. His fangs retracted rapidly, leaving behind the anticoagulant that formed as they had extended. His lips pulled hard on the flesh, forcing blood up and out of the piercings and into his mouth. He gulped the crimson liquid wildly, driven by starvation.

If there was a groan or a scream, he didn't hear it. He felt no resistance. He was keenly aware that had there been, his hunger would likely have led to him tearing out the throat.

His universe became overwhelmingly red—violently red—and it was only when what entered him began spreading through his body and mind, replenishing shrunken cells, that he came back to himself enough to try to bring some level of control to bear.

When he finally but reluctantly was able to pull back from the fountain's source, his vampiric vision left him shocked to see in the darkness of this stone vault who he had been draining: Queen Blanka. Sovereign of the Sapiens realm from beyond the western mountains and to the north. The one who had sat across a table from him just a few nights ago at the conference of vampir and Sapiens heads of state. The gathering *she* had called that was intended to forge communication between the various realms of predators and prey. Where immortals and mortals met for perhaps the first time ever to try to find a way to share the planet without constant, savage warfare.

"So much for diplomacy," he said to the limp body he held in his now-strong arms.

That she was even here amazed him, as much as his own incarceration left him baffled.

He lifted the comatose Sapiens and with his revived energy carried her to the small wooden berth attached to the stone wall of this narrow prison cell.

She was tall, just shorter than his nearly six feet, but her slim frame felt feather-light to him.

A flash-memory exploded: carrying another female body, as light as this one, but he could not recall when, where, who or why. It was common enough to experience trace memories of another existence, but he found them frustrating.

He lay the Sapiens Queen down, brushing the coppery strands of hair back from her flawless, pallid face. It was a face he had been attracted to the instant he'd seen her at the conference. She sat directly opposite him at the eight-sided table. And his reaction to her had surprised him. In his hundred and twenty years in this altered state, he had not found Sapiens particularly alluring, other than for their blood. Usually he viewed them as coarse, their features ugly due to twisting emotions which often belied their true thoughts and feelings. Their bodies seemed overly full to him, as if they had too much inside their skin, and he had always been more than happy to alleviate that condition by siphoning out some of that precious liquid.

But there she had been, her features soft, romantically gentle in a way he may have understood from when he had been Sapiens, her lips generous and well-defined. She moved gracefully, slowly, each action and gesture like a picture she was drawing with her body. She wore a forest-green gown with long sleeves, black lace at the cuffs of her expressive hands and a high lacy neck to her chin—the Sapiens-style gown she was still wearing, although he had ripped away the delicate collar and what remained of the lace was now blood-soaked. Copper lashes and brows framed violet eyes which had looked inquisitive and kind to him, not tainted with the fear and hate usually seen in the eyes of Sapiens, and he had been more than surprised by the attraction he had felt.

At the congress, she'd stared at him once that he'd noticed and held his gaze a particularly long time. He had wondered then if there was interest on her part as well, aside from the polite, courteous and cultured manner she exhibited towards vampirii and Sapiens alike. But he had assured himself that it could not be. It was nothing more than her curiosity at close contact with one of her city's long-time enemies in the same room, he being the enemy closest to her borders.

She was Sapiens, he vampir, and relationships between the two species were uncommon, except for the blood. Those that did come about occurred when a vampir warrior took a Sapiens slave as a personal slave, or more rarely, as a lover. Sapiens soldiers rarely took vampir slaves and when they did, the Blooddrinkers did not survive long.

But she was not a slave, she was a Queen, and that was exceptional in the Sapiens world, which insisted on male rulers. Since he had been King, hers was a city with which he'd had little personal contact, although he had led raids over many decades. He knew few facts about her dynasty but had heard some gossip over the years. Yet, it had been her efforts that had brought about the meeting of vampir and Sapiens rulers two nights ago.

As he looked down at her unconscious form, he imagined she would now regret that initiative.

He checked her pulse to be certain she still had one; he had taken much, and quickly. He lifted an eyelid and the memory of eyes the color of the darkest lilacs resurrected, irises that were now rolled up into her head.

He thought that had he known, he could have controlled the drinking better. But he realized he was deluding himself; he could not have controlled anything. Two nights of starving had left him rabid. She could have been anyone, or even an animal. Anything with blood pounding through veins and arteries. He wouldn't have known or cared, but he did now.

Her pulse was weak but not too irregular, her flesh cool to the touch, but not as cool as his own. The blood-coated skin of her exposed neck betrayed tiny bumps—she was cold, a state that he, like all vampirii, rarely experienced. There was nothing to cover her with. He had only the outfit he wore: the metallic kilt-like skirt of the vampirii nations and not even a warrior's banded shirt, because he was King of his realm and did not require such, just matching black metal bands that crossed, reflecting his authority.

Feeling the sun threatening to take the sky, he lay down beside her on the narrow cot and pulled her body close to his. Facing, on their sides, he wrapped both his arms and legs around her, knowing his flesh was only slightly warmer than the air in this damp dungeon.

He did not know if he could warm her enough. But then, maybe it didn't matter. If she died, it would be a blessing for her; she would not need to suffer further at the hands of their jailers—or at his—because he would be hungry again and could only control his appetite so long. And she, beauty that she was, possessing the sweet temperament and acute intelligence that he had witnessed at the conference and had been so attracted to, a Sapiens ruler with the best of intentions on a planet of rogues, she was the only warm blood around. In the end, it would come down to her existence or his.

Chapter Two

Blanka's eyes fluttered open to a dim grey light emanating from what appeared to be a narrow rectangular window with vertical metal bars near the ceiling. Her vision was blurry and took minutes of blinking to clear.

The vague light, though, was enough to show her two things: she was in a filthy, cold and damp prison cell, which is why she was shivering, and her body was locked in the grip of a vampir caught in his daily death sleep, which could also be why she trembled.

She remembered this vampir from the conference. Thanatos, King of the vampir fortress which, like her realm, was west of the two mountains. His stronghold was further south, but the closest to her city. The vampirii that preyed upon her citizens.

The conference had been the first time she'd laid eyes on him, although her soldiers and his warriors had fought many dozens of battles over the centuries the matriarchs of her family had ruled, making the two of them enemies—but clearly not her only enemy.

She had heard much about him. Rumors—mainly from Sapiens who had been captured and then escaped the vampirii stronghold. Thanatos was new to the throne, just one exceedingly-long Sapiens lifetime, no more. His fight to rule had been ferocious, violent, and some vampirii had left his realm to join another.

She remembered studying his face at the congress. He appeared intelligent and not quite as pompous as some of the other rulers, both vampir and Sapiens. For some reason she felt that he was honorable, although they had not said one word to each other apart from a brief and formal greeting at the start.

The vampirii were handsome males and beautiful females—it seemed to be part of their transition from living to whatever entailed this mystifying state they dwelled in that occurred when they'd morphed from mortal to virtually immortal.

Thanatos was not an exception to what she called the *loveliness of the vampirii*, what most others of her species deemed hideous. Their pale skin and intense eyes she found intriguing. She had never witnessed it, but had been told that vampirii possessed wings and could soar to the clouds. That astounded her and piqued her childhood fantasies of wishing she could fly.

But seeing close-up Thanatos' enormous soft-feathered wings, the shade of deep midnight—even furled, they took her breath away. His relatively expressionless face did not trouble Blanka; for some reason, she found that minimal emotional expression restful. And she admired his noble bearing, as she did with all the vampir rulers—at least most of them. Not every ruler at the conference had struck her as noble.

But at that congress, Thanatos' striking amber irises encircled by obsidian rims and dotted with the jet pupils of his race had caught her off guard. He moved with the mesmerizing fluidity of a dancer. She had not expected to find any specific vampir so attractive that she felt a stirring in her body. She knew they possessed the ability to enthrall mortals, but did not sense that energy coming from him towards her. The erotic response emanated from her and she understood that it was not likely reciprocated.

Blanka had observed him surreptitiously. She sensed his balanced mind and he seemed ethical and direct when he spoke to the group, both what he said, and the way he presented it. By the end of the conference she entertained the notion that he might be an ally in her attempt to bring the two species together.

Suddenly, she had been surprised to find him watching her watching him from across the table. She felt embarrassed and thought of turning away, but didn't. She had wanted to smile, and probably should have, but wasn't sure of protocol in the world of Blooddrinkers. Such an action might be misconstrued as confrontational in a meeting filled with cautious if not downright hostile leaders.

Now, she was alone with him, a vampir, bound by his limbs, and she felt nauseous, her head light. She struggled to remember how she had gotten here.

The last thing Blanka recalled was being dragged from the room where she had been detained for two nights with the day between, when everything had gone terribly awry and slid rapidly downhill at the end of the congress.

That room was much better than this cell, though. Larger, cleaner, and warm. She'd had some food and water, at least until last night, and had been able to move around. But the door was locked from the outside. The lights were on constantly, day and night, and she had been sleep deprived until she didn't know the hour, or whether the sky was light or dark.

Held against her will, both Sapiens soldiers and vampir guards had questioned her incessantly. Her outrage did not seem to affect her jailors.

Ultimately, she reached a confused state and wondered if they had drugged her. She hoped she had not divulged any important information, although she couldn't imagine what that might be. But she also couldn't imagine why she had been taken prisoner, and in the conference center she'd had built!

It must have been last night, she thought. She recalled that she was dozing when suddenly three guards—vampirii—entered the room and pulled her to her feet, then quickly dragged her down two long, dimly-lit corridors. She was tossed into a dark room where something she couldn't see had attacked her. She hit a wall of pain and rapidly-expanding weakness and passed out quickly.

Despite being locked in the embrace of what was deemed at best a semi-dead being, she was able to wiggle a hand to her neck. She felt dried blood and two holes. This one, this King Thanatos, had taken her blood! He must have been starving to do that. Unless she'd misjudged him. Clearly, her assessment of many things had suffered of late.

He was wrapped around her tightly as if trying to keep warm. But her research had assured her that vampirii did not need warmth to the extent that Sapiens did. She thought that he might be trying to keep *her* warm, but she had no clue why until it occurred to her that maybe he wanted to preserve the remains of a meal for a second night? That thought chilled her.

His flesh was cold and rigid. She listened carefully, trying to detect breathing. Vampirii breathed, but not nearly as often as Sapiens, or so she'd learned. Their hearts beat slowly, even slower than a prime athlete at rest. He would wake, and soon, if that paling light fanning through the small window was an indication of the time—nearing dusk, and soon to be dark.

His vampiric vision would allow him to see her in the dark, but she would not see him, leaving her at a disadvantage. At his mercy.

She turned her head to look around. The room spun and she gasped.

Struggling for balance, Blanka tried to breathe steadily through her nose, but it took time for her brain to clear of the whirling, her stomach to unclench from the nausea, and her heart to cease its anxious fluttering.

This cell was small, no more than twelve by nine metres, with high stone walls and a hard-packed dirt floor.

There was nothing in the room but a wooden platform she guessed could be called a bed of sorts. It was less than a metre above the ground, but narrow—more like a bench—and although they were both on their sides, it barely contained them.

The ceiling was high, with only the one window letting in fading light and cool air. And a door that looked incredibly sturdy.

This was not a good situation and after what felt like forever in captivity, Blanka envisioned being neither released nor rescued. In fact, circumstances had gone from bad to worse and she could readily see herself as a daily meal for this vampir until her body was emptied of blood.

The moment he stirred, she turned her head back slowly to avoid dizziness, finding their faces only centimetres apart. The grey light from the window was enough to see that his eyes were open, those strange vampiric eyes; she remembered their color as amber circled by a black ring, the small, dark centers reminding her of insects imbedded in resin.

Now, she watched his irises shift color and darken, likely to red, but she could not see the color clearly in this light. The shift unnerved her and she felt her pulse quicken. She had learned in her research that changes in vampiric eye color meant danger for Sapiens.

"It's night," she blurted out, hearing her voice quiver, stating the obvious, afraid to say what was on her mind, about blood.

Suddenly his irises lightened. He removed his arms

and legs from around her and got up from the bench.

She turned onto her back too quickly and cried, "Oh!" holding her head with both hands as the darkening room spun wildly, and she struggled not to vomit.

"Move slowly," he advised. "It's the blood loss. Unless you've also been starved, as I have been."

Eventually she managed to sit, fighting wavering vision and a lurching stomach. She swung her legs over the side of the bench and bent forward, her head almost on her knees. "I wasn't starved," she gasped, "until last night."

"I was," he said.

"I understand," she told him, and he felt uncomfortable, knowing he shouldn't, because he couldn't have done anything else but take her blood.

"Queen Blanka, I did not know it was you. And I had no choice," he said.

"I understand," she said again, which made him feel worse.

Finally, she was able to sit upright, swallowing air in what he would have called gulps. Her face was ashen, her violet eyes and copper hair in sharp contrast, making her look like a ghost to him. Haunting and haunted.

"This is all my fault!" she said, pain streaking her face. The sky had darkened enough that he knew she couldn't see him, but he could see her very well.

"Who has done this to us, King Thanatos? And why?"

"I do not know, Queen Blanka. When the conference ended, I came down to this lower floor accompanied by my second and third and two other vampirii. I was informed the nourishment you offered we vampirii was below; I needed refreshment for the flight to my stronghold. When we reached this room, I was attacked by all four, including my most trusted warriors. This is my third night here."

"I too was captured at the end of the conference, by a Sapiens and a vampir. Both questioned me non-stop, the Sapiens guard during the day, the vampir guard at night. That's the only way I had any sense of the time."

This struck Thanatos as strange. "What did they ask you?"

"They wanted to know about the defences of my realm, but the questions they asked were nothing important. They wanted to know what everyone knows: Where is my Queendom located? How many citizens live in the city? How many soldiers? How did I come by my title? These are questions that made no sense to me. Most of that information is known to Sapiens and presumably vampirii as well, and none of it is classified. When I questioned their questions, they wouldn't answer me."

Thanatos thought about this. That information *was* well known. It seemed to him like a diversionary tactic. Or more, a stalling tactic.

Finally he said, "I was not questioned. Since I've been imprisoned, I have seen no one of any species until just prior to sunrise last night."

She looked shocked. "I don't understand this." Then, "Do you think the other rulers have been imprisoned as well?"

"Possibly," he said, addressing what he could, "though not likely. King Moarte would not be, I'm fairly certain. As the conference finished, he left before most of the others. And King Hades also left the conference early. I cannot speak for the Sapiens."

"I hope you're right, King Thanatos," she said. She looked down at her hands. "I made such a mistake, trying to bring together all our realms."

He felt sorry for her. This abduction was the result of her desire for peace. It had not been a bad desire, but even he had known that there were elements in both worlds that wanted nothing peaceful to happen. Even now, his warriors would be preparing to rescue him. Or would they? Their King had not returned, but his second—now in charge—and his third could have told his troops anything. His war council, surely they would know something was wrong. Unless they, too, colluded.

As if echoing him, she said, "My generals will be very worried about me. A dozen of my soldiers guarded the conference center, and I brought pages along. They should all have reported back by now, although it's possible they were delayed."

"More likely killed," Thanatos said, and that sobered her.

"My Minister of Security will no doubt send someone to check on the situation and..."

She stared in Thanatos' direction and said, "There will be war, won't there?"

"Yes. There is no way to avoid it. And some at the congress believe in war. It's what Zaget and Lamia both stated would be the indisputable result of the conference."

She seemed startled for a moment, then smiled ruefully. "Wasn't *I* misled! I saw that as only a surface resistance—they wouldn't have attended, otherwise." She paused. "I thought they were the enlightened two. Zaget, a trusted representative of King Zador, and the vampir Queen Lamia he invited to the conference, friends, an inspiration for the rest of us." She looked up in his direction again, struggling to see even the vague darkness of his form.

He read the pain on her face as she said, "King Thanatos, I am so naïve."

He sat next to her. "Not naïve, Queen Blanka, hopeful. It's why we all accepted your invitation. Most of us, anyway. The vampirii are tired of war. Your citizens, it must be the same. Your proposal was good, to initiate talks. But there are those among us—of both species—with other agendas mostly hidden. But by incarcerating at least two rulers, they are inviting conflict of the worst kind."

She was staring at him without seeing him except in her mind. Her startling eyes like lilacs blooming in the darkness drew him. He wanted to move close enough to smell her sweet scent, but knew that he would smell her blood, more than he already did.

When she reached out in the darkness to touch his arm, he snagged her wrist by instinct, his taloned hand tight as a metal cuff, preventing the touch, which he would find invasive and an affront.

When her hand, finding nothing, relaxed, he released her.

"I'm sorry," she said, her head turned down towards her lap again, as if she was looking at the hand that now rested there, a wayward child that had misbehaved. "I…I'd forgotten about touch. I don't understand some of your protocol. I've studied what information is available, but I'm still unclear on some of the—"

"We need to get out of here," he said suddenly, jumping to his feet, knowing that if not tonight, soon, he would be taking her blood again.

She looked around the room, not seeing it except as an image in her memory. "How can we escape? There's a door. Can you break through it?"

"If I could have, I would have," he said a little sharply, worried about what would happen if they were trapped here together another night.

"King Thanatos, forgive me. I'm so sorry I invited you here, only to be imprisoned—"

"Stop!" he said, angrily. "This is *not* your fault and you must stop. This constant self-blame will not help us find a way to escape."

She took in a deep breath and in the exhale said, "You're right, of course. I'm just feeling weak. Overwhelmed. Guilty. Sorry for myself. But this isn't helpful."

Something in her drew him, something beyond the blood. But this was neither the time nor the place. His hunger would rise quickly. Despite what he had taken last night, he now needed more. Much more. What he took had only whetted his appetite.

Suddenly, a key snapped open the lock on the cell door...

⌖

To continue this story, pick up a copy of *Abduction of Two Rulers* at your favorite on-line or brick & mortar bookstore.

About the Author

Nancy Kilpatrick is an award-winning author who has published 23 novels, over 220 short stories, 7 collections of her stories, and has edited 15 anthologies, plus scripted graphic novels and written and compiled the non-fiction book *The goth Bible: A Compendium for the Darkly Inclined* (St. Martin's Press). *Thrones of Blood,* Vols 1 to 6 (Crossroad Press) is her newest series of non-sparkling vampire novels for adults, recently optioned for film and television. She lives in lovely Montréal and enjoys travelling the world—aka the Great Curio Cabinet—ferreting out oddities of people, places and things. If you'd like to get in touch, connect with her here:

Facebook: nancy.kilpatrick.31
Twitter: nancykwriter
Blog: nancykilpatrickwriter.blogspot.com
Instagram: nancykilpatrickauthor
Join the *Newsletter,* once a month & brief. Sign up at the top of her
Website: nancykilpatrick.com

Also from Baskerville Books:

Wild Hunt
by
Nancy Kilpatrick

Do You Know Me?
by
Caro Soles

www.ingramcontent.com/pod-product-compliance
Ingram Content Group UK Ltd.
Pitfield, Milton Keynes, MK11 3LW, UK
UKHW041820200726
13854UKWH00001BA/140

9 780981 324944